A Barnyard Bestiary

For Adrien
DB

Dedicated, with love, to my parents, Ruth and Bill
KA

POEM BY

PAINTINGS BY

A Barnyard Bestiary

DAVID BOUCHARD

KIMBALL ALLEN

ORCA BOOK PUBLISHERS

We are voices from the barn
And we're putting them on notice.
Why is it that they don't see
When we're right before their eyes?
Why is it that they don't hear?
Might they care to see our portraits
That they'll want to show their children
When they ask what we were like?

We are voices from their fields
Who have lived our lives through centuries,
And endured and served them well
Without fame, with little glory.
We've been right here by their sides,
In their yards and leaning sheds,
And we're here because they brought us
And we're here because they made us.

They have always looked with marvel
At our cousins in the wild
That they find much more appealing
For their wit and for their senses.
Yet we too have all that they have
If they cared to look more closely.
They might find us quite attractive
If they took another look.

If they gave us half the time,
Then they too might come to learn that
Like them we have all survived the
Test of time — that makes us special.
And that they again might need us,
No one knows what brings tomorrow,
We might once again be sought for
Various traits they can't foresee.

If they care to stop and look,
They again might come to know us
And they'll find that we're romantic
That we're all *one of a kind*.

In fact if they start to see the
Many things that make us special,
I dare say there might be changes
In the way they live their lives.

Highland Cow

They will find me in the Highlands
Near a slough if I am lucky
Standing knee-deep in the water
And they'll think I'm killing time.

I'll be chewing on my cud,
Something sweet and quite familiar,
Staring blankly into space
Simply waiting for the rain.

In the reeds that sway beside me
To the dry grass on the hillside
All above the roaming, dark clouds
And no need to seek out cover.
That's why they've come to keep me
I'm equipped like so few others
For the rain and bitter cold wind,
For the snow and chilling frostbite,
For the long and dreary dry spells
In the scorching summer sun.

And they kept me for my diet
That is varied more than others.
That by leaving me to graze
I will clear most weeds and brush.

If they think I'm merely standing
Out here chewing, watching time fly,
Would you tell them that I'm thinking?
Would you share our well-kept secret?

How if they learned to smell the rain
Through bending reeds and raging clouds,
I'm sure they'd drop the things they're doing
And come stand by my side.

GOOSE

I had better speak up now
Before they find my voice annoying
They'd be quick to make things happen
That would leave me as a mute.

You think this wouldn't happen?
That my voice must serve a purpose?
That it's only part of nature?
Who has given them the right?

If this is what you're asking then
Consider all the changes, how
They've come to make me look and feel
Like something that I'm not.

The mere fact that they can find me
Near them summer or in winter
Tells the drama that I feel
When I can't fly north or south.

Yet I dream I'm somehow flying
Near the clouds, toward a mountain
Looking down at those below me
Who have always wished they could.

Yet I dream I'm somehow flying
It seems ages since they've let me
Since they banned me from the sky
Does this seem natural for a bird?

(Is it right that I abandon
That I'm somehow stopped from brooding
That my eggs mean oh so little
What more is there to my life?)

In fact if I should be grateful
To all those who've tried to shape me
It is for the trait they've mastered
I'm now starting not to care.

Buffalo

I have reason to be bitter
More than most of those around me
Yet I focus on the future
In the hope that they have learned.

I pray that what they did to me
(That's archived in their history)
Has taught them something they will use
And not repeat today.

I pray they've learned their lessons well
Of how the plain had been *my* home
Before the tracks of iron were laid
Before they brought their guns.

We all died almost instantly
For meat, or fur, or tongues or teeth
For sport, they liked to call us game
Then stacked our bones in piles.

(They must have found another need
To drag me from my prairie for I'm
Wakened from my nightmare
Standing in this farmer's field.)

And now I'm in these pages among
Those you call domestic asking
What they have in mind for me
And what's come of my home?

Onagadori Chicken

When the great Lord Yamanouchi
Second Baron of the Kochi
Sought out plumage for his standards
To impress the mighty Shogun,
Sought a bird with wondrous feathers
There were none like *me* around.

When in 1655
The actual task of my creation
Went to Riemon Takechi
He found none at all like me.

So he sought out the Shokuku
Who could boast a three-foot feather
Up to three feet if not longer
Who would flaunt his fancy plumage.
But he found with the Shokuku
That for all his given beauty
It was only momentary
That he molted every year.

What if somehow the Takechi
Was to breed a master chicken
Who could keep his first grown feathers
For the ten years of his life.

What if somehow the Takechi
Found the secret of this molting,
Somehow came to breed a show bird
Who'd add three feet every year,
Would the Emperor not be pleased?

Thus the essence of my story
And the pleasure that you bring me
That by telling of my purpose
That by showing them my beauty
That by paying me this tribute
You bring honour to my Lords.

TURKEY

When pilgrims landed on the rock
They found but one domestic bird
The same one that Ben Franklin chose
When others picked the Eagle.

We all ran free and foraged hard
For meals of seeds and berries
And required little care to move us
From their yard to table.

But over time in trying their best
To make us that much fatter they laid
Out a plan not giving thought
To that of Mother Nature's.

Our chicks who once were hardy little
Fighters now are coddled for they
Haven't the resistance to fend
Off the morning's chill.

Yet as they age they should become
Much better at survival, that by
Running and by hiding and by
Flapping hard their wings, they should
Find a spot just out of reach
Of dangers that are lurking.

They can't, of course, they're weighted down
By meat, their breasts are swollen,
Thus they cannot fly, can't run nor hide,
Can hardly bear the bulk.

We even now depend on them
To breed, that's right, to stay alive
With this I'm sure you'll understand
The reasons why, as time goes by,
Once every year, we too rejoice
When comes Thanksgiving day.

Jacob Sheep

If we're looking for an angle
That might capture their attention
I have seen the look of shock
When they're told that I'm a sheep.

Amazing how their vision works
That makes them point each time they look
In my direction, toward my horns
It seems to help them count.

It's somewhat less than fortunate
Their color sense is less refined
I've heard them say while watching me
That sheep are black or white.

You'd think that over time they'd learn
About my wondrous fleece and horns
You'd think that over time they'd see
The many kinds of sheep like me
You'd think that over time they'd change
They've not since Jacob made his choice
Of spotted sheep in Laban's flock
The Bible says it's so.

SCHWARZHAL GOAT

If my friend from in the valley
Tries to capture their attention
With his charm or with his history
With his multi-horned charisma
With this feature hardly noticed
We'd do well to let him go.

If my friend however seems to
Want to focus on his color
Seems to want to draw attention
To his fleece, more than the other
I should stand up now to speak as
Mine is obviously superior
To all other sheep and goats and
That's as clear as black and white.

I too was once endangered
When I thought my days were numbered.
Though I'm hardy and I'm thrifty
Though I've been a part of history
As a goat They were expecting
Much more milk than I could give.

But I'm working on a comeback
In the Alps, almost in heaven
On a green Elysium meadow
Where a gentle wind doth blow.

Donkey

Read the Good Book for my story
That's been told for countless centuries
Of the services I rendered
To your king when he was born.

Ask his mother whom I carried
Of my special place in history
Of the animals around you
Ask her which one *she* prefers.

Then explain to her the changes
How today I'm much less needed
Transportation and the tractor
How my time is drawing near.

And explain how they've created
Sanctuaries for this poor beast
Who is battered and neglected,
Who of those who shared the manger,
More abused than any other
From my birth until I die.

And her answer, I have heard it
In a stable spoken softly
Will for me, if I am worthy,
Be a place beyond the clouds.

SHIRE

If romantic and nostalgic
Are the banners you are seeking,
If aesthetics and sheer power
Are the values that have meaning
If the times I risked my life for you
In battle or while laboring…
You'll want to take a moment
And give thought to what you're doing.

My knight would know just what to say
If he were here with me today:

"Draw swords, you knaves, prepare to die
If ere I hear that you neglect
My wondrous steed who's saved my life
And those of countless kings.

Must I return through centuries
Of rest and sleep to fight anew
My own descendants who have shown
No valor, pride nor shame.

Through battle he has carried me
Done all and more than any beast
Thus carved his place in history
Draw Swords! Prepare to die!"

Blonde Mangalitza Pig

You'll undoubtedly have noted
I was not bred for my beauty.
I expect you will agree that
There are few who look like me.

And you're right if thus you see me
I'm a curly-coated, fleecy pig
Your eyes are not deceiving you,
I am a pig and not a sheep
The last one of my kind now that
The Lincolnshire's gone.

I'm very large and quite rotund
A pig that offers ample lard
A substance they use less today
And thus no need of me.

I somehow thought, don't think me crass,
That my uniqueness might just find
Me of some interest to your kind,
Aesthetics seem to please.

I somehow hoped I'd fascinate
The few who care for rarities
The few who understand "extinct"
Means now until forever.
That *you* might understand "extinct"
Means *I'll* be lost forever.

Ostrich

If all these things we hear are true
Of careless, cruel and thoughtless deeds
And those to blame are trying to hide
Their heads deep in the sand.

If all the things we hear are real
Then let *them* hear a voice or two
From those of us so far from home
Now living on their land.

I can't assume that they all know
Just who I am or where I've been
And just because they've brought me here
I can't assume they care.

I'm proud as Jacob sheep to have been
Mentioned in the Bible and
Delighted, like the donkey, with
A special few who've ridden me.
I'm somewhat like the shire horse
With speed much like a cheetah and
More handsome than that hairy pig
Though not to say more dear.

I know your interest is my egg,
My meat, my skin, my feathers and
I'm ready to be bound to you for this
And much, much more — But please
Tell me that the things they say
About your cruel and careless ways
Are nothing more than idle talk
Mistakes and bad folklore.

BORDER COLLIE

Don't be cross to hear my voice
Among these others who accuse you
As I've been throughout our history
I am always on your side.

Don't be cross to find my portrait
Among those you've disappointed
As I've done throughout our history
I'll be always by your side.

But my kinfolk have a reason
To be mourning many losses
To be thinking of the morrow
To be planning for a new day
To be hoping that in some way
When it comes, they'll have survived.

And I tell them how you've labored
How you've worked, just how you've struggled
How you've learned to be resourceful
Using every part of nature
How success has somehow taught you
That the world was meant for you.

Then I tell them how in spite
Of these successes you have always
Kept a warm spot right beside you
For me, always by your side.

How could one so soft and gentle
Be found guilty of not caring
Not be willing to stop hurting
Not be willing to start learning?
And to teach you, they should let *me*
After all who could be better
Than the one that from your own mouth
You have always called "best friend"!

They've accepted that our senses
Are in many ways superior
To the gifts that they were given
By our mother "the Good Earth."

They've accepted that we're brothers
And they use the word quite freely
When it serves them for their purpose
You can call *them* animals.

But the gift that they have mastered
That has made them feel superior,
That has made the world their playground
Is that they can somehow speak!

If *we* could, they'd have to listen —
And we'd ask what they are thinking
When they use us and abuse us
Do they think that we don't feel?

Watch your dog express his sorrow
Or his pleasure when he greets you
Do we have to speak in rhythm
Lest you see that we have soul?

If they haven't come to notice
Then it's time they start reflecting
On all those who'd like to speak
To be heard, just one last time.

If they haven't come to notice
Some are only here in memory
Some gave everything they had
And deserve some thanks and praise!

To the cattle "Irish Dunn"
One of Ireland's finest dairies
And the curly Lincolnshire
Less than thirty years been gone.
To the Horn ram from Norfold
Or the Sandy pig from Oxford
To the hundreds of lost breeds
We would want them all to know:

That although it's taken time
Some seem ready now to listen
And although it's been too long
It appears that some *do* care …

That we've done as we have said
We have shared the words we spoke of
And we'll know how well they heard
As we watch them live their lives!

If they care to stop and look,
They again might come to know us
And they'll find that we're romantic
That we're all one of a kind.

In fact if they start to see the
Many things that make us special,
I dare say there might be changes
In the way they live their lives.

Canadian Cataloguing in Publication Data
Bouchard, Dave, 1952 –
A barnyard bestiary

ISBN 1-55143-131-9

1. Domestic animals – Poetry. 2. Domestic animals in art.
I. Allen, Kimball, 1952 – II. Title.
PS8553.O759B37 1999   C811'.54   C99-910035-1
PR9199.3.B617B37 1999

Library of Congress Catalog Card Number: 98-83004

Orca Book Publishers gratefully acknowledges the
support of our publishing programs provided by the following agencies:
the Department of Canadian Heritage, The Canada Council for the Arts,
and the British Columbia Arts Council.

Design by Christine Toller

Printed and bound in Hong Kong

Orca Book Publishers
PO Box 5626, Station B
Victoria, BC Canada
V8R 6S4

Orca Book Publishers
PO Box 468
Custer, WA   USA
98240-0468

99 00 01   5 4 3 2 1

The original paintings presented in *A Barnyard Bestiary* now reside
in the collection of West Coast Reduction Ltd.